RAILWAY LINES: VIEWS FROM A COMMUTER

Mark Rasdall

Copyright © 2025 Mark Rasdall

All rights reserved

The characters and events portrayed in this book are fictitious. Any similarity to real persons, living or dead, is coincidental and not intended by the author.

Published by Burwell Web Communications Ltd

No part of this book may be reproduced, or stored in a retrieval system, or transmitted in any form or by any means, electronic, mechanical, photocopying, recording, or otherwise, without express written permission of the publisher

CONTENTS

Title Page
Copyright
Rights   1
Introduction   2
Morning Olympics   4
Security notices   7
Late arrivals   9
Beginnings   12
Tickets   14
Parking   17
Glasses   19
Noises on   21
My office   23
personal space   25
inclement   27
diy   29
Vision but not visionaries   32
Say it out loud   35
Don't panic   38

You are what you eat	40
Wake up: children	43
Winning isn't everything	46
Brakes gave us all a break	49
Some like it hotter	52
It's all for the best	55
Not My Fault	58
Royally male	60
Uniform	62
Insight	64
Music and movement	67
Floods	70
Travelling post office	73
Renovation	76
Allergy	79
Commonwealth	82
Brunch	85
Charge	88
Happy new year	91
United	94
Election	97
News travels	100
Lobsters	102
Extraordinary, darling	104
Centre court	107
Hairy journey	110

| Mailing List | 113 |
| About The Author | 115 |

RIGHTS

Text

This is a work of fiction. Names, characters, businesses, places, events and incidents are either the products of the author's imagination or used in a fictitious manner. Any resemblance to actual persons, living or dead, or actual events is purely coincidental.

INTRODUCTION

In 1993 we moved as a family out of London and back to my country roots in Cambridgeshire. Born and brought up in Peterborough – on the other side of the county – I had been used to train journeys down the 'main line' from home to King's Cross. Cambridgeshire 'boasted' some of the most densely packed commuter trains in the country and yet Littleport station, when I first used it, was little more than a concrete platform with a tiny waiting room which was always closed and locked. I never did see any bodies in there, but there may have been…

I commuted by train from Cambridge and Ely in East Anglia to London for some 25 years and this is a collection of humorous observations on train travel and railroad travellers. Volumes One and Two are also available individually on Amazon as digital downloads only.

These sketches are borne mainly out of frustration with railway travel but also a fascination with seemingly limitless English eccentricity. Railway officialdom, passengers and unexpected situations are described in satirical fashion including ludicrous questions asked at the ticket office; the commuter who insisted on setting up a mobile office environment; the eating habits of a bearded explorer, not to mention former actors, high-powered executives and ladies who lunch on each other's weaknesses.

Some of these stories were first published online in Cambridge News.

MORNING OLYMPICS

The 6.45-morning train from Cambridge to London King's Cross usually ambles on to Platform One at about 6.30 so there is ample time to select practically the seat and carriage of your choice. The train is now twelve carriages long once the second half arrives from King's Lynn, so you can walk almost to the end of the platform and still find yourself pleasingly aligned to a train door.

Unfortunately, commuters, smarting from the previous evening's home run, still see this as some kind of early morning competition. Occasional travellers are scorned by the regulars for being unfit and not having made the required training sacrifices they have committed to over so many long years.

It was raining so I sheltered under a platform shelter, adorned by posters urging me to consider moving to Cambridge, until the train came in. The instant I emerged, I was jostled by what seemed to number several hundred athletes, panting loudly in their matching yellow tracksuits, all following the yellow line at the platform edge and refusing to give any ground on the inside of 'their' running track.

I then got stuck behind three burly railway workers in high

visibility vests who formed a human wall which any high jumper would have struggled to clear. They were talking knowledgeably about the Hertford Loop, which I have often been forced to follow too, but only as an untrained amateur, obviously.

I eventually found a window seat on the platform side and watched the assortment of shuffling, walking and running techniques, each favouring sticking-out-elbows to avoid being overtaken.

The doors closed with the familiar message, suitably muffled and barely coherent: 'In the interests of safety please remain seated while coupling operations are completed' followed by the door alarm.

A young woman with jet-black hair and jet-black suitcase leapt through the air and just managed to avoid the closing doors, herself, and her suitcase landing with a thud in the carriage. I saw no red flag so assumed all was fine until she started to shout at her family party who remained on the platform, each with a similar line in jet black branding.

"Quick. The train leaves..." she yelled.

I instinctively knew that she wasn't talking about the autumn leaves that were more akin to Winter Olympic sport on the railways. It was also August.

"It's OK," I left my seat so that she could see that the soothing message came from a fellow competitor and wasn't just a voice in her head, "they are just connecting another train to this one..."

She moved backwards, warily, so I followed her, slowly, whereupon she threw up her arms as though I was trying to kidnap her and had paid First Capital Connect to provide the getaway train.

"Don't worry, this isn't Rio!" I tried to make light of the situation.

She looked puzzled. "I know this," she replied with a conviction, previously lacking, and "there is no beach."

SECURITY NOTICES

Not a lot of people know this but there is a 'magic eye' on all First Capital Connect trains – a bit like those invisible devices in hotel car parks which know you're approaching and cause the barrier to 'automatically' rise at the last moment (unless you're driving a battered old car that doesn't fit the demographic of the guests they'd like to be entertaining, in which case there's an armed security guard with special access to a manual override).

On the trains, it's a sensory device that somehow knows when a passenger has closed their eyes. At that point either a ticket inspector arrives, as if from nowhere, or the public address system goes into spasm and starts spitting out all kinds of useful messages very loudly.

"Please keep your personal belongings with you at all times" – almost always results in elderly passengers glancing up at the overhead luggage racks every thirty seconds or so, in case burglars or SAS units swing through impossibly small cracks in the windows, on ropes, and crawl towards coats or bags quite undetected.

"Please be careful when alighting from the train" - this one always plays just after the doors have closed. It's probably operated by the cousin of the security guard in charge of hotel car park barriers.

"Please do not block the aisles" – a personal favourite of

mine on evening trains back to Cambridge when you can't actually see the aisles for swaying bodies.

"I'd like to remind passengers that there are safety notices situated throughout the train; if you get a chance please familiarise yourself with their contents" – this just proves that all train drivers really fantasise about being airline pilots, in the same way as London Underground staff wish they were running the railways. The tell-tale signs of the latter include staff directing people to 'Platform 1' or 'Platform 5' rather than Victoria Northbound or Piccadilly West which would be a bit more consistent with the tube map, signage and how the average person uses the Tube.

Back to railway drivers who long to escape from the sidings of their lives: if they had their way, there would be short safety films embedded into the back of each seat. Animation - or maybe even a suitably tattooed colleague with sympathetic voiceover - would take passengers through the imminent dangers of getting stuck in the toilet, or the doors or next to someone with a penchant for curry and crisps.

Younger passengers would hunt in packs, up and down the carriages, until they had located each and every poster and answered the relevant questions on paper sheets attached to eye-threatening clipboards; all rounded off with abstract sketches ('it's a work of art, darling') drawn with stubby crayons and received by railway staff with a pride and courtesy not witnessed since Brunel started building bridges.

A whistle blows. The driver reluctantly places a thermos flask carefully back into travel bag; puts on trusty, black-rimmed glasses and we move forward, safely and silently.

LATE ARRIVALS

Unexpected delays on inward journeys: drivers oversleeping; slippy leaves: no, not part of the litany read out in semi-serious voices by train drivers, but reasons that are given by passengers for their own late arrivals at the station.

Running or waddling ungainly down the platform, pausing only to stare through the windows at smug early birds yawning their contempt for their lack of planning, they try to spot spare seats or unoccupied luggage stands.

If they're really late they will hurtle onto the train just in time to catch a vital piece of equipment in the closing doors door such as umbrellas which must stand taller than the Shard and wider than the Welwyn tunnel when fully extended. This, of course, delays them even further, not to mention everyone else.

Some seated passengers swear under their breath, while latecomers generally curse the whole unsatisfactory situation openly and loudly as if it's the fault of everything and everyone other than themselves.

"Wretched driver – he could have waited a moment longer."

"All this effort and now I have to stand for the whole journey: unbelievable."

"The sooner they scrap the A14, the better..."

Others are just plain angry. Seated passengers reading the early morning 'Metro' quietly or ritually checking their mobiles for tests, tweets or messages are suddenly thrust back into the physical jungle. Overflowing coffee cups or 'quality' newspapers are slammed down on flimsy shelves next to them. 'Ordinary' bags and coats in the luggage racks above them are thrown roughly to one side as very important briefcases or executive suitcases are hurled into the parking spaces obviously (though secretly) reserved for their betters, accompanied by huffing and puffing commensurate with such blatant insubordination.

Eyes bulging out of reddening faces distorted by rage, it is clearly expected that 'the ranks' will move from aisle to window seats to make way for their superiors. Most do nothing of the kind, choosing to sit their ground. A key driver for them getting to the station early was to secure aisle seats in the hope and expectation that they will not then have to endure anyone sitting next to them – especially not tiresome latecomers - at least until Royston.

They are the 'residents' and latecomers are entitled only to view the land next to them, not seek to occupy it. It is a ridiculous argument of course and easily solved by questions, posed with a level of sarcasm correlated with the number of degrees at which the seated passenger's head is turned away from the enquirer, and no more complex than

"I assume you've paid for two seats?" or

"If you don't mind, I'd quite like to sit down too."

There then follows the wearisome spectacle of passengers sitting on the aisle pretending to move their legs out of the way and the invaders deliberately catching them with their own trailing feet or taking as long as possible to complete the maneuver.

'Sorry for the delay.'

BEGINNINGS

When I'm travelling to London my day begins at 5.20 when the mobile goes off. I am usually passing through a quite different world at that time, where railway companies pride themselves on the cleanliness and timeliness of their trains; astonishingly, people are also treated with respect and called 'passengers' rather than 'customers.' Naturally, this is turning into a bit of a nightmare but thankfully the incessant ringing intrudes on my dreams and helps to deliver me back into the real world.

I usually then spend several minutes wondering where the sound is coming from and why nobody puts a stop to it, before realising that it is a 'phone – my 'phone - which I answer when it and I are aligned in the same direction. Obviously, there is nobody there because some fool who looks remarkably like me in the wardrobe mirror had merely set the alarm function the previous evening, never expecting to talk to anyone that early in the day. I eventually remember how to switch it off, check for messages and bury it under the pillow, hoping it won't go off again, ever. At which point I often do, which is why I also set a proper alarm clock, timed to go off five minutes later and which is horribly reliable.

I shave, shower, somehow find myself in the kitchen, and head for the kettle, occasionally filling it with water before switching on. I then remember to park my car at the station, which is a remarkable achievement given that I'm still standing in the kitchen and the car is sitting patiently outside. I try to 'phone RingGo but realise that I can't, not because I can't remember the number but because I can't remember where I've left the mobile.

Waking everyone in the house up for a second time due to putting on lights, tripping over the cat on the stairs (however did I manage to miss it the first time?) and opening drawers and assorted pockets of jackets I couldn't ever remember wearing, I recognise the usual hiding place and head back downstairs again.

Parking, tea, and bowl of cereal behind me, the village soon is too. I listen to the BBC News then switch off quickly before Vanessa Feltz tries to turn me on again. I cannot stand her voice. Back in my dreams, she would be tied to the track, and I would be the engine driver.

After numerous near misses with ambling pigeons in Swaffham Prior and speeding drivers who don't understand the traffic lights in Lode, I arrive in Cambridge and on to Mill Road. There, I must swerve to avoid racing cyclists who think that lights are an unnecessary weight handicap, enlightened delivery van drivers who take great delight in parking on the wrong side of the road and dazzling all oncoming traffic with their lights left on full beam, and numerous potholes cleverly designed to ruin all car suspensions.

Brand new days; same old beginnings.

TICKETS

You wouldn't think that buying train tickets would be that difficult, would you? I mean, much as I love the song, I think Diana Ross was fundamentally wrong and that most of us do know where we're going to - at least as far as railway journeys are concerned. Add in the ability to pay for the tickets to take us to our chosen destinations and it should be plain sailing (perhaps that should be railing?).

Queuing up in the mornings at the ticket office at Cambridge Station, waiting patiently to buy my ticket, it is often unclear whether my fellow would-be passengers really understand that both of these are quite important.

The men and women manning the ticket office can appear to be quite cross or even scary, but I have learned that they are actually really friendly and willing to help. 'Enquiries' from the general public have just ground them down and, unlike me, I suspect that their capacity to be unduly surprised has long since been diminished by the quite extraordinary reality that they have witnessed on the other side of their windows.

There is a 'travel centre' but, even when it's open, it uses a supermarket-type ticket system and drives most people bananas. There are also the ticket machines but 'you just can't reason with a machine, can you?' I have heard each of the following, without any embellishment on my part:

"What will the name of the engine be today?"

"How do I get from Heathrow to Kennedy?"

"If a man has six oranges and three lemons..."

There are the very important travellers, of course, who only listen to their own questions (expressed at maximum volume, or so it seems at that early hour) and none of the answers:

"What? What? Speak up, I can't hear you! Well, why didn't you say so? I can't stand here all day you know: I've got a train to catch."

The ubiquitous overseas visitor, with three generations of family and corresponding suitcases accompanying them, effectively seals off the entire area more effectively than police tape or traffic cordons ever could:

"We don't wish to travel to Liverpool Street we need to go to London."

"Can we take our luggage with us or does it have to go ahead by freight?"

There is the privileged, minor aristocracy (in their Debrett's-induced dreams) who know nothing of the hours of the day or days of the year but whose expectations are great and understanding of the rest of us waiting in the queue are small:

"If we were to take a train to Peterborough, what do you suppose would be the chances of making a connection to the north, assuming we'd ever want to go there?"

"I'm afraid you must be mistaken. Return tickets to Stamford cannot possibly cost that much. We were at

Burghley only last year, you see, and the cab from the station cost less than that! Would you mind checking again?"

Tickets to rile...

PARKING

Engine drivers never have problems parking their trains. They have signalmen and points to guide them into sidings which are never occupied by other trains. They won't find engines or carriages double-parked, making it nearly impossible to open their doors, let alone move forwards or backwards, and they won't get stuck in queues. When it is their time to be run into sidings or engine sheds, that is the time they park. When the allocated time comes for them to move out again that is the time they leave: no obstacles, no hassles. There may be a bit of rusty reluctance in the early mornings but that's enough about engine drivers.

For commuters, it's quite different. If driving to the station, there is a need to park somewhere – anywhere and we are treated simultaneously with open commercial arms and weary contempt by the 'authorities.'

I sometimes travel from Ely station which is almost impossible to park at during the week unless you have a season ticket or drive a milk float, with your round finishing there in the middle of the night. Most occasional users have to use the 'overflow' car park in Angel Drove which in reality means a long wait under the railway bridge behind articulated lorries waiting patiently to cross the tracks or inarticulate van drivers who either cannot read or think that 'low bridge' warnings do not apply to them. Angel Drove is only a short walk to the station, but Tesco is situated between the two and shoppers delight in trying to run down three commuters for every two they aim at.

When I commuted from Littleport there was free station parking for a while which always resulted in a mass scrum at the end of each working day with tempers and bumpers frayed by the experience. They then built a new car park, boasting a tarmac surface and which of course you had to pay to use. My car was broken into twice there, proving that it offered real values for money.

Cambridge station car park is, of course, a model car park, as you'd expect would be provided from such a busy, world-famous university city. The planners have clearly modelled it on some kind of chaos theory - probably substantiated via all-expenses-paid trips to the great driving behaviour capitals of Paris or Rome.

The 'station quarter' is being re-developed but not the car park. Bus stops are situated at the car park entrance, providing maximum danger for zebra crossing users. The guided bus terminus has replaced the short-term version opposite which means that short-term, car rental but also longer-term parkers are all guided to a 'dedicated' section where they vie with each other for space (assuming they bypass the cycling mafia first). None can get out again in the evening until 'main' car park users, taxi drivers, Swiss Dry Cleaning patrons, parked police cars (like their owners) or Biffa recycling lorries say they can.

New quarter provided? No quarter given.

GLASSES

Google - famous for search and online maps that work - is sponsoring a new research initiative called 'Project Glass.' Its aim is to develop a head-mounted display (HMD) based on augmented reality. Effectively this means a pair of glasses that enable you to receive and read texts and e-mails in the same way as you might do on any other 'mobile' device such as a tablet or Smartphone. This information would appear in the top corner of your 'screen' a bit like rabbits racing into your peripheral vision just before you curse and swerve to avoid hitting them in the very-nearly reality of your own twilight zone.

What's not clear yet is whether those of us who already wear glasses for a living will be able to have their vision enhanced for a hefty fee (no research is really free) or whether we'll just have to be content to see the world as it really is. Many rail passengers are already frustrated by being unable to see into the future and, clearly, see glasses as a cause rather than a solution to their problems. They are regularly pushed up on noses which were there first and thus the glasses have to fall or gradually slip into line. They are hurled with dramatic flourishes on to airline-style coffee trays as if to make an example of them - and their owners - until the sticky remnants of previous occupants' spilt drinks highlight the lack of vision behind such attention-seeking exercises.

Large women without the foresight to wear tight clothes which they can be poured into but never sit down in without displaying their culinary past, wear their dark glasses high on sweaty foreheads as style accessories accompanying hair by Peroxide or scalp by Mr & Mrs Druff and their errant son Daniel.

Beady-eyed men stare furtively at younger girls' skirts, not realising that their bifocals fool nobody, all of us reading the signs while they pretend to read. Older people stare at newsprint that grows smaller by the day, their pupils enlarged by lenses and stories that grow bigger with tabloid imagination.

Nervous people clean their glasses continuously as though they have finally decided to face their futures and remove any grey areas of worry, before removing their glasses once again as the outside world appears to be, well, just too real.

Dishevelled passengers carry extra breakfast supplies on their lenses and rims while romantics form their own wet patches from reading too many 'heart-warming' tales or listening to ABBA songs from the later years on iPods or, incredibly, successfully interpreting tannoy messages from the driver whose private life is more off the rails than you'd realise.

This reality is all around us and needs no augmentation. Many people can see without the need to search; can communicate without the need to be connected. All of our lives are terminal but not all of them need to be dominated by them, whether or not we are mobile or happily grounded.

NOISES ON

As in so many public situations, there are lots of occasions where groups of people individually make noises rather than conversation.

A short, stocky Asian man frequently gets my train and follows the latest news stories from the Far East on his iPad throughout the course of our journeys into London together. I know this, not because there is any audible narration but because he provides his own 'oooh' or 'ahhh' conclusions depending on whether it is good or bad news. I know this not because I can read Cantonese but because I have deciphered other verbal clues and worked the correlation out for myself. I suppose that's what comes of being an inquisitive writer.

A middle-aged white man with torn off punk T-Shirt, leather jacket (even in the middle of summer) and Elvis Costello glasses often sings to himself - and us - as his wraparound headphones would otherwise block out that particular enjoyment. He's no more in tune than Stiff Little Fingers were but his version of 'Alternative Ulster' would have put the Good Friday agreement in severe jeopardy. He's happy even if we aren't.

An orgasmic reaction of 'Oh my God' from a young African woman with more hair on her head than was biologically possible broke the early morning silence a few weeks ago. The shriek caused heads to be turned or slowly appear above seat backs down the entire length of the train: tired faces suddenly wide awake and hoping they might witness the re-making of a famous movie scene. Sadly, for all of them - and especially the poor young woman - it was more like 'When Harry's half-full coffee cup fell off of the table and met Sally's dress, pouring it's piping contents all over it and her.'

There are many occasions where 'silent assassins' are discharged from the travelling public producing cries of barely concealed dismay from other passengers. The guilty parties usually feign the same kind of disdain but if that doesn't give them away, furtive shuffling in seats confirms it. Less silent versions can, of course, be pinpointed with the accuracy of all-knowing human radar. The worst I can remember was the sound of a low whining noise, like a piece of machinery that had just been switched on and just went on and on. The perpetrator simply stared at me, daring me to comment or react in some way which of course I didn't, given that I could barely breathe at the time.

Other noises include barking sounds, sometimes from dogs, enthusiastic 'Hey' greetings when people answer their mobiles like later-day versions of The Fonz and, of course, the mobile 'phone tones themselves. The best (worst) for me was a sound like a sneeze. On the fifth 'atishoo' I got up and offered the recipient a handkerchief - to form a kind of shroud for her mobile, protecting it until it's death would be discovered long after I'd thrown it out of the carriage window.

MY OFFICE

One of my earliest railway commuter memories was of a middle-aged man creating a working environment on the train which was for him and him alone.

He was middle-aged, well-nourished with bulbous red face and long white hair - rather like our perceived views of what a scientist should look like when not surrounded by test tube chaos and other visual clues. I assumed that he worked at the Science Park and made regular trips to London to sell his medical breakthroughs to a city community which scoffed at the prospect of taking its medicine and preferred to take his money and run. We now know this to be called 'banking.'

Our scientist had one of those bulky laptops from Toshiba with the little mouse wheel device attached to the side. It was probably state-of-the-art at the time but, of course, without any internet connection to the outside world. Not that our man in IT Heaven would have noticed this. Like his computer, he was sitting in a standalone bubble and never responded to fellow commuters' pleas to sit in adjacent seats or to stop jabbing them in the arms as he endeavoured to test the non-laboratory mouse on another new document or spreadsheet.

One day he went a stage further and introduced a portable printer which sat proudly next to him - a long umbilical cord enabling the laptop to give it life, which turned out to be a noisy one. Dot matrix computers never came with their own sets of user headphones - not even when Apple converted these sounds into rap music and sold them via iTunes.

Many passengers, therefore, got quite emotional when asking him to move the offending device but got responses based on hard logic such as:

"If I moved it, I'd need to find a perfectly flat surface and WAGN (yes, it really was that long ago) don't supply them in their standard coaches, only seats" or

"How can I read what I've written without printouts?" or

"This is important work; I'd love to spend my journeys listening to music too, but my boss is impatient for results" or

"If you worked as hard as me, you'd be able to afford a First-Class seat and no doubt have more room."

The irony of that last one was not lost on them or me but whereas I simply observed, they resorted to schoolboy tactics such as accidentally pulling out the printer cable when he wasn't looking or knocking the mouse off through some intensive leg or arm crossing.

I thought about him again yesterday as I typed this out on my iPad, headphones plugged in and listening to the playlists I'd synched with my PC over the weekend. Technology has moved on but I'm not sure he will have done. For most of us, small, discrete devices are what we crave - with minimum exposure to or disruption of fellow travellers.

I later learned that he was, in fact, a priest.

PERSONAL SPACE

Many years ago, when I first started commuting by train from Littleport to London I became much more aware of the importance of personal space when travelling.

I had of course taken many journeys by train, especially as a student when journeying fairly frequently between home in Peterborough and university (and football team) in Leeds. On many occasions I had to physically push passengers further inside in order to climb onto the train itself, never mind the puissance of cases and bags and rucksacks to be vaulted. It was bad at the other end if others had subsequently managed to get on at Doncaster or Wakefield and created their own layers of chaos.

At least one less-than-bright spark would usually pipe up with some original comment such as 'Where's Jimmy Saville at times like this?' in reference to his 'age of the train' advertising campaigns and being a Leeds resident too. I think we all know the answer to that question now...

Commuting is a bit different in that there don't seem to be too many students around at 6.45 on weekday mornings – unless they've overdone it and think they're still on buses travelling down Hill's Road to some late-night party from which they really don't wish to be woken up. I do see a few of those. Mostly, though, they are regular, hard-bitten workers who doze quietly or leaf furiously through newspapers quickly and loudly, representing as they do really bad news from yesterday and the suggestion of worse to come today.

Recently a bleary-eyed, chunky man with suspiciously populous beard plonked himself beside me and proceeded to push me further and further towards the window. I hadn't seen him before so assumed he either knew nothing of personal space or was worried that passengers of a similar build would knock into him when passing down the aisle. Naturally, I pushed back and made sure he was seated much more precariously by the time we got to Letchworth. I had The Clash on my headphones at the time, which helped.

I witness a lot of similar nonsense with people whose width is vertical. Impossibly tall, like characters from Tim Burton's latest nightmares, they bend long, gangly necks around doors and perform strange crouching maneuvers beneath the luggage racks – I assume out of fear that they may come face-to-face with the remains of a dead giraffe which forgot to duck.

Commuters who travel in 'a four' (two seats facing two seats with a small table between them) are the worst. Usually, one very important businessman or woman seats themselves in one of the aisle seats and stretches their legs out in front of them. Not only does this make it difficult for parents with small children to get to the window seats but it means that the commuter, disgruntled at having to share their established empire, then resorts to 'accidentally' tripping up the young revolutionaries on their way down the aisle to the toilet.

INCLEMENT

Collins defines 'inclement' as 1. (of weather) stormy, severe or tempestuous 2. Harsh, severe or merciless

I can honestly say that I only really hear the word used these days in tannoy announcements at railway stations: 'Due to today's inclement weather, please take extra care when travelling along the station platforms and concourse.'

Concourse? Yes, formal language lives long and hard on Britain's railways behind the hi-tech new roofs and floor to ceiling windows that let light but not enlightenment in.

Because of the adverse weather conditions (have I caught the bug too?) I've been hearing these messages a lot this week. It's been freezing on Cambridge station in the mornings and foggy on several return journeys, but I wouldn't say it's been harsh or severe and 'merciless' probably only really applies to station managers insisting on running the message on the loop so that you hear it several times while waiting for your train to actually arrive. Punctuality is clearly secondary to meteorological scaremongering.

People do listen though and some take notice. I saw a middle-aged woman walking gingerly along the yellow line in a chilly remake of 'Don't step off of the crack or you'll fall into the sea' on Tuesday. On Wednesday several international businessmen re-enacted the lunar landings of the early 'Seventies as they alighted (another favourite railway word) from their carriage slowly and deliberately and made their way to the exit with greatly exaggerated high steps - all beautifully choreographed in slow motion to hold everyone else up while they performed.

Remember the sketch where Rowan Atkinson arrives at a restaurant with a coat draped over his shoulders? The waiter takes it from him only to reveal a jacket similarly loosely hung. I saw a very large, elderly man give us his own take on this recently. Slowly removing a life-threatening Fedora to reveal a rectangular, bald head, he looked every bit the Bond villain as he climbed into the carriage. He then removed the huge black overcoat that was draped over his square shoulders (there were no soft curves in this man's life) to reveal a short-length jacket in matching black, similarly draped. He took this off to reveal yet another black item – a quilted waistcoat which obviously hid his gun and holster just below. He didn't speak so I couldn't confirm that he was Russian, but he was much more Octopussy than octogenarian in terms of a threat when bit part actors tried to join him on set at Royston or Letchworth Garden City.

Some passengers, who have dutifully heeded the warnings, forget them as soon as they get on their trains. One teenage girl was so pre-occupied with her Smartphone that she slipped right over in the aisle but kept texting without breaking concentration (or, hopefully, bones) while another kept opening the window to further enjoy the Arctic air. Needless to say, this action was shared on social media for much longer than it was by her increasingly tempestuous followers.

DIY

Like everyone else, I was heartily sick of the advertising campaigns over Christmas that promised relaxing holidays for 2013. They implied that this was a stressful time and that we would all deserve good breaks as rewards for coping with friends and family by showing, er, friends and family but just eating and drinking in different locations. These included exotic destinations such as the Maldives or islands in the Mediterranean or the many familiar tastes of Blackpool: our own island of dreams.

It reminded me of the 'Skegness is so bracing' ads that previous generations of escapists grew up with. Rarely do holiday ads make it to railway carriages these days. Unfortunately, the ads for home improvement products (did you know that the average total usage of a power drill over its entire life cycle is only twenty minutes?) and assorted furniture soon replaced the holiday campaigns on television and those, sadly, do still appear on trains and, worse, in true 3D format.

Two female DIY disciples from Letchworth spread the good news to the rest of us on Wednesday in better than Dolby 5.1 surround sound, or so it seemed:

"So we went down B&Q and they said they'd replace it!"

"What, satin finish?"

"Better than that: textured satin AND quick-drying backing. We were well chuffed."

"Unreal! So how did you spread?"

Many crossings of legs at this point and iPods surreptitiously paused.

"Well, you know me and bristles…

"Oh what, like those little hairs left behind in the whole sticky mess?"

"Like that was so not me this time, though. Apart from some flappy bits that got stuck in my hair I just smiled and let it happen."

"Not like me then. I couldn't get the spout out."

"Not cool!"

"Yeah. I was so careful. They say you have to tease it out gently or it will just run everywhere before you're really ready for it."

"Those caps have got a lot to answer for if you ask me. How were your ridges?"

Crumpled newspapers hastily placed on laps and spilt coffee wiped up self-consciously with tissues.

"Didn't feel a thing and you know what it says on the label!"

"I never really look at the labels, to be honest, just slap it on and hope it doesn't come off before I've finished. Found a really cool scraper, though. It's got like a cutter at one end and brush at the other."

"Best not to get it the wrong way round then…"

And so it went on, and on ... We additionally learned that papering ceilings was particularly tricky after a few drinks down the pub and pattern matching wasn't necessary at all as 'nobody looks that closely, do they?'

As we drew into King's Cross, exhausted, and overloaded with useful tips and advice, I longed to see a platform hoarding which would take me away from all of this but the only exotic destination being promoted was a tannoy voice announcing the next departure for Letchworth.

VISION BUT NOT VISIONARIES

I have worked in advertising for many years and, some years ago, two of us were travelling to a meeting in Manchester together. We were on a packed Virgin train from Euston and all kinds of conversations were taking place around us.

My colleague had previously worked in the research department at Granada TV, then a key ITV franchise holder. Whether keen to ignore my wittering on or just curious about a particular conversation I wasn't sure, but he tuned in instead to a key strategic plan for one of that company's advertising clients being relayed to us in fairly minute detail somewhere between Milton Keynes and Crewe.

He was horrified at the carefree sharing of confidential information in exactly the same way I imagine he would be today with sharing of social and financial information on 'free' WIFI networks where the true cost can be identity and data theft.

I thought about this earlier in the week when sitting just behind two civil service types on my journey into London. In our village of Burwell, we have been discussing, as a community, a 'Burwell Masterplan' put forward by East Cambridgeshire District Council for some months.

Bizarrely, after much feedback and dialogue, the council officers then presented a replacement 'Burwell Vision' document instead.

The two travellers were talking about something similar:

"We did everything required of us so they can't complain now." The elder man was tall with short grey hair and wearing an expensive-looking dark suit and overcoat and pink, silk tie. He spoke in an 'I'm in control of the situation,' assured tone – no doubt honed after years of debate squashing.

His colleague was younger and squatter with displeasing acne marks and a tendency to squint each time he started to talk. He too was dressed a little too expensively, so I assumed they were local apparatchiks on a day out to the big city rather than worn-out commuters who had stopped trying years ago.

"Absolutely. What is their problem?" Junior was trying to sound grand and mocking but came across as a poor actor in his first run-through of a play at the local Rep.

"Village-types always expect us to change things as a result of their putting forward their views. We've had a listening brief on this one for quite some time."

"GCHQ?"

"Of course. The Highways people ran a traffic congestion model and estimate that traffic at Quy will be up by 50% in ten years. It will soon be worse than on the railways! Had to be in the consultation document of course but down towards the rear as some might say."

"And our people are certain they can quell this…"

"Democratic expression? Of course. Everyone wants nice houses in the country. That's what East Anglia is all about these days. We're not going to buck that trend are we?"

I sat back realising that they were about as strategic as semolina: tasked with a vision but certainly no visionaries.

SAY IT OUT LOUD

It's a well-known fact that English commuters are known to be tight-lipped, tolerant in the face of ridiculous adversity, courtesy of the train operating companies, and infinitely polite. They are also very, very quiet.

This is even more prevalent on the London Underground where the mix of cultures and nationalities is like a mobile United Nations app where you get to burrow under the great metropolis, scoring points with each Tube stop you reach but losing them if you foolishly say anything out loud.

The early morning Cambridge to London trains are normally packed. Even with the extra four carriages, people are often standing before the trains leave Cambridge and definitely after Royston. There must be some law of probability or scientific principle that says the greater the number of tired, disgruntled people you can pack into a metal container on wheels, the more likely it is that one or more of them will talk to each other, or to themselves.

I haven't noticed any great increase in conversations, which continue to be frowned upon (as a constant in the equation) but there are definitely more singularly vocal passengers.

Not all of them are barking mad either.

Last week a large woman with moon-like face supporting more slap than a baby's bottom during a midwifery course, plonked herself down next to me. When I'd caught my iPad that had jumped up from my knee with fright, I turned to see that she was wearing a severely cut, dark business suit with a sensible white blouse and one of those civil servant identity tags around her neck. It sported a glamorous face shot which bore no likeness at all to her true, unlovely self.

"I hope you're not going to make a racket with that keyboard!" she boomed at me, waking the old man opposite with a jump and causing the coffee cup of the young girl in front to edge away from her across the tiny seat tray.

"Of course not; the keyboard is on silent," I responded in similarly brusque fashion and at the same unnecessary volume.

"Just keep your fingers quiet then."

I suspected then that she was either jealous of my having an iPad; bored to tears with her paper-pushing role in Whitehall, or plain deranged.

"I'll do my best," I sniffed, "but idle hands make the devil's work."

She wasn't impressed and proceeded to squash me against the window.

"Spare me your trite responses."

As if in preparation, she fell asleep just before Letchworth. She was snoring by the time we joined the main line at Hitchin – loudly, obviously.

Then, just after we came through the Welwyn North

tunnel, I thought I heard a whispered announcement from the driver and strained to hear more. Noticing that nobody else was doing this I realised that the words were coming from the lovely, Collagen-induced lips to my left:

"Tickle me. You know where I like it best."

I kept my hands firmly to myself.

DON'T PANIC

As Corporal Jones used to remind his fellow platoon members and us every week, there was an absolute requirement not to panic when faced with adversity, while showing us outwardly that everything was relative.

Railway commuters traverse the adverse nature of the British railway network every day and face more trials than Norman Stanley Fletcher did in 'Porridge.' It isn't just the theatre of the absurd performed on a set where heating is timed to come on only in the summer months or the lights in the daytime, but also the plots that Network Rail and the train operating companies direct for our benefit and how our characters individually and collectively respond to them.

I remember travelling with several Romany families (no point in flogging a dead horse) towards London when the driver announced over the speaker system that our train was due to arrive in Liverpool in approximately forty minutes. I'm still not sure whether it was the prospect of a liaison with Liver Birds, lack of time to prepare for the traditional reception at the station ahead or the fact - duly verified - that each one of the parties had simultaneously heard voices in their heads that accounted for the panic that ensued. Babies in multi-coloured jackets were passed from women to men to children to sleeping dogs and back again. Bundles of clothing and baskets of food (most of it dead) were hauled from the overhead luggage compartments amid much-excited chattering and frantic battering of windows and doors. All to no avail of course as the train drew into Liverpool Street thirty-nine minutes later to the relief of the travellers and perhaps disappointment of the driver.

Only this week, my train came to a sudden and unexpected stop at Stevenage station. Now, there's obviously nothing especially remarkable about halting in Hertfordshire and timetables are as much an approximation on railway journeys as the availability of seats or clean toilets. However, we hadn't been due to stop there and the 'hidden clock' to which commuters' and fat controllers' hearts tick was disrupted.

"Why are we here?" asked one sleepy philosopher, woken from the expected assurance of an uninterrupted run from Letchworth to King's Cross.

"Where are we?" asked a young woman to nobody in particular, including the person on the other end of her mobile 'phone signal who had, like us, enjoyed a blow-by-blow account of her life since Royston. This must also have been a rhetorical question as the 'Stevenage' sign actually blocked our view of those passengers on the platform who wanted the train to move out of their way as much as we did, given the doors remained closed and every minute of our delay would postpone their own train by at least an hour.

"Nothing to worry about" the grey, besuited passenger sitting next to her reassured her as he placed his headphones in his ears once more, returning to a place where life was once less scripted.

YOU ARE WHAT YOU EAT

Railway commuters give us insights into their true characters in a variety of ways. Verbal and non-verbal clues are made available so that we can define and then describe who our fellow passengers really are.

I've been captivated by MasterChef recently and one of my favourite clues is, therefore, the food and drink we consume while travelling and the way in which we do so. Unfortunately, the actual experience of it isn't always my favourite time spent in a packed carriage.

As the trains rush frantically towards their man-made destinies, so human beings seem hell-bent on rushing towards consumption.

On one journey last week I watched a trendy young thing perhaps eighteen or nineteen years old - consume a bar of chocolate and three packets of crisps before we'd even left the platform at Cambridge. On his penultimate packet, he started to cough (a crumb of discomfort I suspect) and sprayed little bits of potato over the seats and the seated all around him. I waited for him to profess a public apology between attempts to take in vast crisp-flavoured lungfuls of breath but, no, we just got a discordant 'oh, hell' delivered in a very posh voice.

From this I deduced that we were in the company of either a very hungry or very greedy student to whom table manners didn't apply when sitting behind a mere table rest and for whom collective responsibility meant a rather tedious dinner party or patronising referral to 'the masses' one had read about in one's history tutorial between snacks. Not so much a golden wonder as a tarnished walker.

A bearded explorer for whom middle age was also history climbed into the carriage at Royston, bringing with him mud, damp hair and sweaty clothing for free - selfless sharing of his love for the environment if you like? I didn't and quickly ascertained that his stained windcheater had probably been retrieved from the same putrid bog he had cleaned his teeth in that morning. He cheerily produced a family-size Tupperware box, filled with a small mountain range of brown bread sandwiches containing presumably more remnants from his bog findings and accompanied by a bunch of discoloured carrots that would not have been seen dead in a Tesco 'washed and peeled' collection.

Like our student friend he had obviously been away on some long, historic expedition because he could barely consume his victuals quickly enough.

'Wot larks eh Pip?'

'Er, I think you may have already eaten all the wildlife in the surrounding area, Joe.'

I heard belches from the seat in front of me as an exceptionally well made-up young woman discovered the buck in Starbucks and then a noisy and extended breaking of wind - possibly from the next carriage - as that special passenger endeavoured to put spice into all our lives.

As they say on MasterChef 'that's a beautiful thing!' For me, beauty is in the eyes and ears of the withholder.

WAKE UP: CHILDREN

It's bad enough to have to get up at 5.15 in the morning and drive to Cambridge station to catch the 6.45 to London but at least I've usually had a decent night's sleep and don't fall over toys, bikes, and weird objects I swear I've never seen before on my way out of the house.

Our children are much older now. Different kinds of nocturnal activities still wake us up in the middle of the night but clearing up sick or 'definite' sightings of ghosts are mainly behind us.

It's a shock, therefore, whenever my early morning train carriage is invaded by families containing small children. Normally, a passenger having a coughing fit is met with knowing tuts of disapproval or frowns that could tell their own stories of pent-up frustration or reveal the very real likelihood of extreme violence. Faced with young children at that time of the morning it's amazing that this toxic combination doesn't deal with falling infant mortality rates at a stroke.

Pale and exhausted parents that I recognise as shadows of my own past sink wearily into seats as far away from their offspring as possible but always get discovered, as they knew they would, amid victorious declarations at maximum volume:

"We wondered where you'd gone!"

"You told us to find seats with a table! We waited for you, but you didn't come!"

Wearily, they sip their coffees, remembering a time about a thousand years ago when Starbucks meant spreading out with a newspaper, music and possibly a muffin. All of those things are still available of course but children's' unique commentaries and interactions on current affairs shout much louder than mere paper words:

"We've just gone over a bridge...we're not going to crash, are we? I can't swim. I didn't like the swimming teacher. You said we'd look for a different one. You're always tired - perhaps you should go to bed earlier too..."

The coffee has almost certainly been spilt over the table, seats, trousers of anyone within fifty yards of the epicentre and the muffin will have been offered as a taster, half-eaten and then rejected with:

"Ugh. How can you eat that? Why didn't you buy a Kwasson? I'm hungry!"

Of course, they have selected the noisiest devices invented by man or Apple for their train journeys: headphones that don't so much leak noise as provide a flood that even Noah would have done well to survive; games consoles emitting noises that only technology could have created, and mobile 'phones with a seemingly infinite range of ringtones to be sampled. I sometimes think I've landed in the middle of some clever crowdsourcing project, targeting the youth market. But that's marketing speak so how could it possibly be real?

"Turn that down please; there are other people on the train apart from you."

Such appeals are, of course, turned down even more noisily.

I may be more sympathetic now, but I was never in tune with these symphonies.

WINNING ISN'T EVERYTHING

Commuters rarely speak to each other. Sometimes they talk to themselves and even argue out loud the competing points of view in their heads, but rarely do discussions take place that the rest of us can listen in to and have our own silent points of view on.

So, when common issues of the day do arise regarding politics or transport or the economy or transport or sport or transport, there is a curiously intense interest in what is being said.

A large, sweaty lady, dressed in a bright blue matching anorak and eye shadow had just such a conversation with a thin, pale boy in jeans and a tee shirt (probably twenty-five years her younger and almost certainly her son) one bright morning this week. They got on the train talking in loud, authoritative tones before she plumped for the window seat (I had an uncomfortable vision of what plumped up cushions must look like on her settee at home) and the boy follower sat almost next to her but more on aisle than seat.

"You can quote records at me all you like but it won't make any difference." she sniffed as she awkwardly removed her azure outer garment to reveal strangely incongruous pink tracksuit below.

Perceptible groans were heard as we all thought that, at any minute, he was going to mouth off about Dizzee Rascal, The Script or The Emperor's new Rhianna before treating us to tinny, extended plays of each, via noise expansion headphones.

"Stats don't lie," he began, at which, as one, we metaphorically shrugged in highly superior fashion and awaited an oral dissertation illustrating the ignorance of youth, "he won the U.S. and would have won in Melbourne if he'd have got the breaks."

"But that's just it. He didn't make the breaks when he should have! It's no good having set point if you're essentially a jelly, is it?" She started to unwrap a slab of chocolate as the young lady opposite pulled her knees under her chin to avoid those tell-tale brown signs on her cream skirt.

"You'll see, "the boy was undeterred, though he did glance around at us, seeking moral support at this point, "taking a rest from the French will prove to be a blessing…"

None of us could really argue with the latter point.

"He's improved on grass and clearly loved Queens…"

'We might be needing Hawk-Eye after all,' I thought.

"And, as long as he doesn't do his back in again, or meets Nadal too early…"

"Ah. Excuses already!" brown sludge appeared at the corner of her mouth and dribbled down her chin, just as she thought she'd put the last volley cleanly away.

"Andy Murray will win Wimbledon."

"Not even if Camelot offers it as part of a National Lottery draw he won't. He's an unlucky player."

The boy smiled, his service game over. "We may not agree on everything, but it was a lucky match for me, the day I met you."

BRAKES GAVE US ALL A BREAK

I remember watching Casey Jones and his Cannonball Express when I was young. I loved those adventures, especially in what seemed like almost every episode when the vast steam engine's brakes would fail and the whole train was heading for imminent disaster before Casey worked his magic and saved the day – yet again.

The Railway Children was one of my favourite ever films and I loved the scene with the landslide where only Jenny Agutter's red knickers seemed to come between the inevitable, disastrous pile-up and unexpected salvation shot in soft focus and with that haunting soundtrack in the background.

Readers will spot some common themes here: steam trains, prospective railway disasters and possibly a misspent youth in the late 'Sixties and early 'Seventies watching TV programmes and films about trains. Another is brake failure and impending doom as a result.

This week we were sitting on the 6.45 from Cambridge which begins as an eight-carriage unit before being joined by its cousin from Norfolk to form a twelve. We didn't leave at 6.45 or 6.50 and, just before the 7.00 news could report it on the local travel round-up the driver decided to tell us what had occurred.

"Good morning, everyone. This is your driver speaking."

Now, it isn't just commuters who would understand that the voice on the passenger announcement system is likely to be the driver unless the driver had been kidnapped by some kind of local terrorist cell from Foxton or Shepreth that didn't know how to drive a train. So, impatience with the delay had already turned to the much more toxic noun of 'frustration.' It would take something authoritative and believable to diffuse this.

"I'm afraid that I have some rather bad news for passengers: the brakes on this unit have worked."

This was not the explanation we were seeking.

"They have stuck fast; therefore, we cannot proceed."

What would Jenny have done? Presumably, she would have kept her knickers on for once and in early preparation for an acting role as a nun-cum-midwife some forty years later. Had it been Casey and we were watching repeats on Sky the solution would have been simple: rewind.

"Of course, it had to be the front unit!"

If he was pausing for laughter at his ironic comment, he had underestimated the audience sitting behind rather than in front of him. Each of us found ourselves looking from speeding watches to any kind of sharp implement we could find...

"So please can customers pass down the train into the back eight carriages so that we can be on our way."

It wasn't clear whether the passengers who had dared to sit

up front were the problem or, indeed, whether the driver was leaving for an early breakfast.

Twenty-five minutes later our shortened train hit Royston with the driver apologising for a 'faulty unit' at Cambridge. Brakes eh! Who would trust them?

Well, not Casey or Jenny, that's for certain.

SOME LIKE IT HOTTER

I expected the London Underground carriages to be dripping with sweat because of the hot weather this week. Previously, travelling by Tube in such conditions has been akin to having a warm shower without any soap, leaving passengers damp and some even more grubby on the outside than in. However, whether tourists had been advised to travel by bus to be cooler and appear cool or whether the underground system was working without the usual delays, I found my journeys underneath Central London remarkably bearable.

Walking down Platform Four at King's Cross for the train back to Cambridge last night appeared to be following a similar pattern: reasonably breezy and fewer passengers waiting by faded number fours on the platform's edge. They do this in order to align themselves with the doors of the carriages when they come to a halt at the station. Unknown to them, I'm sure many train drivers watch them in their mirrors, deliberately nudging forward or stopping further back just to watch the collective reaction all along the line...

By the time the train eventually came in I was surrounded by floral prints and cream jackets in various stages of decay. Bulbous faces peered anxiously towards the tunnel beyond for first sight of the train – like the trainspotters they had always been – and then shuffled forward and sideways as they tried to guess the final door positions. Of course, they took no notice of any passengers trying to alight from the incoming train. These included a single mum with pushchair and three other children who formed a human island which then had to be circumnavigated, accompanied by much clicking of dry tongues and other heated verbal abuse.

I managed to get a window seat and was almost immediately joined by a middle-aged man in three-piece cream, woollen suit with an umbrella. He did take his jacket off and straightened it endlessly before placing it carefully in the overhead rack. Unfortunately, tightening his tie and smoothing out his trousers he then realised that the umbrella should have gone up there too. Because his middle-age spread caused his lovely waistcoat to extend into the aisle, this delicate maneuver meant that he blocked all movement past him while he did this. He was also in no hurry and so quickly experienced what it must have been like to be a mum with a pushchair and three other children, travelling on First Capital Connect at peak time.

One tall young girl had spotted a spare seat across from him and, finally losing her cool, pushed past him, causing an unexpected and involuntary pelvic thrust in my direction, before he resumed operations.

Finally, he sat down, sweat pouring from his head and arms and, if not at all embarrassed, certainly mighty red-faced. He proceeded to then lust over the late female arrival as she bent forward to send texts on her mobile, not realising that his choice of camouflage was entirely inappropriate for the occasion.

In 1993 we moved as a family out of London and back to my country roots in Cambridgeshire. Born and brought up in Peterborough – on the other side of the county- I had been used to train journeys down the 'main line' from home to King's Cross. Cambridgeshire 'boasted' some of the most densely packed commuter trains in the country and yet Littleport station, when I first used it, was little more than a concrete platform with a tiny waiting room which was always closed and locked. I never did see any bodies in there, but there may have been...

I commuted by train from East Anglia to London for some 25 years and this is the second volume of twenty-one humorous observations on train travel and railroad travellers.

These sketches are borne mainly out of frustration with railway travel but also a fascination with seemingly limitless English eccentricity. Railway officialdom, passengers and unexpected situations are described in satirical fashion including ludicrous questions asked at the ticket office, the commuter who insisted on setting up a mobile office environment and the eating habits of a bearded explorer.

Some of these stories were first published online in Cambridge News.

IT'S ALL FOR THE BEST

I was on holiday for the first part of August, in a hot Catholic country where infrastructure such as road and railway networks was poor and inefficient. The people who lived there were also incredibly poor and largely uneducated; still suffering from generations of elitist power and, previously, dictatorship.

However, they were invariably kind and attentive, and friendly and always welcoming. With the growth of tourists coming into their country they can see a way out: a departure from the endless spiral of self-serving government, lack of investment and reliance on aid from others. They are optimistic that this is the best route to a better future.

I was still thinking about this when our son's A' Level results came in, just as we got back to England. He did well, and education should make a real difference to his life, allied to the fortune of being born in a 'developed' country.

I also thought of my own A' Levels all those years ago, including French in which we had studied Voltaire's Candide among other texts. Candide was published in 1759 at a time of severe repression of a dreadfully poor people by elitist officials, aided by self-righteous institutions such as the Church.

Candide (also translated as Optimism) is - taking some strands of the Enlightenment movement - a satire of this unfair situation amid the premise that we do all live in the best of all possible worlds.

Catching up on news of more than 4% annual rail increases to come and a post-Bank Holiday emergency timetable to London due to 'over-running engineering works at Alexandra Palace' I put all of these thoughts together into an imaginary carriage scene:

Ticket Inspector (bellowing): "I want to see all tickets."

Poor person in rags (sitting all alone, obviously): "Can you tell me please why the trains are messed up this morning?"

Ticket Inspector: "Didn't you hear the announcement? Perhaps you didn't understand it?"

Poor person: "I didn't hear it otherwise I wouldn't have asked but I'm sure there is a perfectly good explanation for such disruption."

Ticket Inspector: "Too right there is, matey; and not for the likes of you to question it. It's not our fault - we just run the trains as best we can. If the infrastructure's not in place there's nothing we can do about it."

Me: "Apart from charging ever-increasing fares."

Ticket Inspector: "Listen, sir, you're very lucky to have an efficient railway service. We are the envy of many other countries."

Me: "But not all?"

Ticket Inspector: "Some people aren't interested in railways, sir."

Me: "Probably put off by the costs of running them?"

Ticket Inspector: "The paltry fares don't cover the costs, sir. You're one of the lucky ones. All Railway Operating Companies have a certain amount of flexibility in the rates they charge. It could be much worse."

Priest (smugly): "Where there's hope there's holiness."

Me: "Holes in arguments, at least for the enlightened many."

NOT MY FAULT

Have you noticed that when travelling by train in this country nobody is ever at fault when things go wrong or, much more likely, it's always somebody else's fault?

I had a day this week when so many things seemed to go wrong that I began to wonder whether it was my mistake in expecting a good or at least reasonable experience, whereas the rest of the travelling population were expecting everything to be bad and so were quite happy that their expectations were met in full.

Quite unreasonably I hadn't expected the Biffa truck to be blocking the car park that early in the morning. Waste management is important but also wastes a lot of time. I eventually parked and walked briskly to the ticket office. Obviously, I hadn't expected a queue at that early hour of the morning, so there it was, snaking around the marked-out pens that informed railway companies' view of the cattle they were forced to transport.

"You'll have to tap it" the burly ticket clerk informed me knowingly as the credit card machine did its best not to recognise my PIN and preserve my anonymity. "Cheap components you see; nothing I can do about it." He raised a mug the size of a small sink and proceeded to gulp down the hot liquid before proclaiming, as a kind of cheery sign-off, "Even the tea's rubbish here."

I slotted my ticket into the barrier and nothing happened. I was considering whether it had made some kind of infrared pact with the faulty credit card machine when the gate suddenly flew open.

"Software fault!" was the weary assessment of the small Asian man whose eyes were nonetheless completely wired – possibly due to the rubbish station tea. "I've been on to them, and they keep saying they'll come to fix it but they never do..."

"We regret to inform passengers..." was the barely audible tannoy message that welcomed me to the platform. Those five words of introduction are well-known to regular commuters and the harbingers of terrible news to follow such as 'your train has been postponed until a week next Friday,' or 'we won't be stopping at Newmarket today because it's just too dull.'

Today, of course, it was for passengers hoping to leave all of this imperfection behind by flying off from Stansted. Should have gone to Heathrow or even Specsavers because anybody who can read overhead monitors (and station staff frequently struggle with their hidden meanings) would know that it was as much an airport express service as Brian the Snail on speed.

My train to King's Cross usually leaves from Platform One but, of course, that was now impossible as another train already occupied that piece of track and was determined not to be labelled as the 6.27 to Liverpool Street. In fact, it was refusing to move anywhere soon because of an as yet undiagnosed fault. No doubt they tracked it down eventually but as to whose fault it was...

ROYALLY MALE

In the mornings when I'm waiting on Platform One of Cambridge station for the 6.45 to London, I usually align myself with some familiar point so as to know where the doors to my favoured carriage will come to rest (I know: doors close rather than rest but you what I mean).

It sounds a bit grand doesn't it – regal even – to have a preferred carriage? But I do, based on warmth, expected degree of overcrowding and length of walk required at my King's Cross destination. This is what happens when you are a long-term commuter, and we get unreasonably upset if the formation of the carriages changes or the driver tries to catch us out by braking too early...

I usually stand opposite the Royal Mail sign on the vast office opposite the station. My father used to work for the Post Office and took great pride in his role in delivering the mail at all costs, at all times of day and in all kinds of weather. He worked on the old mail trains for some seventeen years; sorting post through the night as the train rattled up to Crewe or down to London or nearby Bury St Edmunds where it would simply be turned around and make the journey back again.

I was thinking about all this yesterday when two burly, middle-aged men in black overcoats bearing the same Royal Mail insignia got into my (our!) carriage with microwave-sized black bags which they threw on to the still empty seats beside them. They proceeded to talk loudly about every subject known to man but definitely not women, homosexuals or anyone born abroad. Loutish and royally rude – even openly obscene – they seemed to think they had taken on the roles of mobile entertainment officers and were, therefore, entertaining as a result.

I have no idea why they were travelling down to London by train – perhaps a shift pattern at Mount Pleasant or maybe a course to re-train - run by Royal Mail in its newly floated guise as a civilised trading partner - and bring its staff into the same Twenty-First Century that many of the rest of us inhabit?

I'm sure my father and his colleagues regularly discussed the popular issues of the day but I never heard him swear and he would have been horrified and ashamed to even hear 'conversations' about sex or race. From what I remember of his workmates I can't imagine any of them talking in such a public way in front of children or families, not to mention the 'weaker' elements of society these two had so much fun condemning.

My father took delivering the Queen's mail pretty seriously. I only remember him ever having one night off work – for flu when he could not stand up properly. To my shame, I did not stand up for him or the rights of all travelling passengers yesterday. I hope the message 'return to sender' will get through eventually.

UNIFORM

I am on a train today dressed in comfy jumper and jeans. I say comfy not in the middle-aged sense so scorned by the younger generation but because it is warm without making me sweat - which fellow travellers might not appreciate - and it makes me feel like me. I am comfortable with both myself and my surroundings. I don't feel the need to wear a uniform anymore.

Of course, there is a real mix of styles and fashions surrounding me and holding my perceived lack of dress sense to ransom but no amount of money would persuade me to re-enter the race for fashionable acceptability.

Several old ladies are off for a day trip - possibly a matinee followed by a nice cup of tea and a scone if the production is good; then safely home. Each dressed in their 'Sunday Best' as my Granny would have described it, this is probably the best they can do now on any day of the week. Once-stylish camel hair, leather, and woollen jackets flit, according to the level of carriage heating, over blouses and pearls of wisdom.

A couple of young girls, barely out of college and barely in any kind of clothing are draped across the table in front of them. Like them, the table has survived yet another early-morning invasion of the coffee cups, but its virgin white facia has long since been stained by carelessness and waste. They nudge each other and wink as the older generation tell their stories, assuring themselves that they will never be part of such ugly scenes.

Young executives, targeting sales for others and sails for themselves, are dutifully dressed in dark suits over pastel-coloured shirts and occasional sharp ties. Their hairstyles vie for headspace and are, alone, worthy of Tate Modern. Smarting eyes glued to mobile 'phones and unhearing ears plugged by iTunes, they proudly wear the costume jewellery of today; until tomorrow comes.

Old men in crumpled anoraks and greasy, slicked-back hair read The Sun loudly. Page after page offers them comforting thoughts that they are not alone and will have deserved the cigarettes currently burning in the inside pockets of their minds: rewards for

making their dull and unprofitable journeys through life. They detest young 'buddies' and old 'biddies' equally, for they were the real 'nowhere men' of the Sixties and still are.

The ticket inspector joins up all of these dots on the train map. Tall and pale, in regulation dark trousers that are too short now and jacket buttons that once met and got on OK together, he still has that hint of teenage rebellion in an official badge that sits at a rebellious angle. His tired eyes have seen hope and despondency, vigour and exhaustion.

"Can I see all tickets please?" is his question. Because of a near universal need to conform, 'where is life really taking us?' is the one you will never find most of us asking.

INSIGHT

The handy thing about commuting from Cambridge is that jolly useful advice and observations from a higher species of traveller are made available, rather generously I think, for free to the rest of us.

One morning this week I was fortunate to benefit from such a philanthropic approach to life.

Two well-dressed middle-aged chaps strode into the carriage and immediately opened the window to allow the raging gale outside to join our party. One of them had an elaborate and very hairy hat, which would have put any member of the Blues or Royals to shame, and which he nonchalantly tossed into the overhead luggage compartment. Unfortunately, there was no overhead luggage compartment - only dim lights to witness the brightness of his intellect - and it descended like a boomerang on to his immensely posh companion's silver flask (thankfully unopened).

"Good shot! Hope you don't peak before New Year's Day..." Much guffawing at high volume followed, obviously, as the thought of systematically killing small, defenceless animals filled them with Christmas spirit.

"Assume you got that SCR business sorted out?" Hat man had been trained to speak in hushed tones when secret codes or acronyms were being deployed.

"Oh, that! Let's just say that I don't expect much opposition to my proposal - not now the pennies have finally dropped as it were..." Shrieking, near hysterical laughter naturally followed such wit that the rest of us could only admire.

"Excuse me mate but could you shut that window. It'll be freezing in here once we start moving."

A brave suggestion from a burly man, standing in the doorway as there was no room in the carriage to sit.

"I'm not sure that's necessarily the case actually." Flask man responded, sniffily. "It will depend on the velocity at each angle of air direction and, as we will not be travelling in a straight line - don't believe everything you may have read about railways - the effect will be one of fluctuation."

The burly man moved closer and bent down to whisper in his ear. We didn't hear what he actually said but clearly, the message of peace on earth prevailed as Hat man immediately shut tight the offending opening.

Flask man rather cleverly changed tack - such is the benefit of an insightful mind.

"I overheard a rather interesting story the other day."

"Unlikely but pray continue" Hat man retrieved an iPhone from his lovely jacket pocket and began scrolling through messages with abated breath.

"Well, it concerned some do-gooder fellow, almost certainly in the Middle East."

"Definitely not Netanyahu then!" Hat man could never have hidden his dazzling conversation pieces under any bushel.

"No, but that does sound a bit like the place he hailed

from. Anyway, it seems he was born in some kind of farm outbuilding and became fascinated by carpentry as a result. Went on to build one of the first churches ever constructed..."

"Lordy! Hope the restoration boys are on to it then; would be unforgivable to forget."

MUSIC AND MOVEMENT

I have always enjoyed music and often write about lyrics that take me back to people, places, and memorable events.

I have background music on as I work – usually an online radio stream or songs from my iTunes account - but sometimes even from physical CDs. Digital music availability also engages a mobile audience like almost no other product and has built on those early Sony foundation days when Cliff Richard told us he was 'wired for sound.' Worryingly for Cliff, our imaginations were stretched almost as far as the early cassette tapes we hooked ourselves up to.

Train carriages have long been a breeding place for passengers to listen to music on the move or be moved to ask others to 'turn it down.' Stropify are us!

My earliest encounter with this phenomenon was years ago when I requested that a young, well-built black guy turn his music down when travelling through Balham on the Tube. I knew no fear in those days, it seemed. He smiled nicely, slowly removed his headphones, and held one cup against my right ear. The shock of hearing Val Doonican caused me to move quickly to the next carriage as the train pulled into Tooting Bec. If I had stayed, I'd have had to request Bob

Marley ahead of Paddy McGinty's goat.

We love to guess what other people are listening to don't we? This is patently ridiculous as music taste follows neither creed nor colour nor social class. For many of us, song selection is based much more on mood and memories than manufactured image. I had a bad day in London recently which instantly got worse when I realised I'd left my own headphones at home:

A white man of Eastern European appearance, possibly in his early 'thirties, had succumbed to the white line of choice in the full gaze of everybody else on a packed commuter train back to Cambridge. His iPod must have been on maximum volume with bass boost on, on, on as we sped through the tunnel at Welwyn North. Either his ears were faulty, or the Apple wiring was as tired as I was because Ian Dury's rhythm stick hit me over and over again.

"Excuse me. Could you turn that down please?"

"Is Ian Dury!"

"Yes, I know."

"Ah. You like?"

"Yes, but not now."

"Why? You only like Ian Dury when he alive?"

"No."

"No! Music helps us to remember I think; much like postcards."

"No. I didn't mean that. I just don't want to hear you playing it right now."

"I not playing it. Not one single bit: Ian Dury playing it."

"Look. I love Ian Dury. I saw him live when I was a student. I've got two of his records..."

"Ah. Vinyl. I thought so. Is making a comeback you know?"

"He can't. He died..."

"Not Ian Dury. You not very bright? Vinyl very popular again now. But this digital recording of course."

Of course, it was.

FLOODS

Two highly important, middle-aged businessmen sit opposite each other on the early morning train; suited and booted and sporting fantastically similar, bushy grey eyebrows.

"Wretched nuisance: these floods!"

"Well, yes, of course, but they don't really affect us do they?"

"Don't affect us? How can you say that?" Beautifully folded copy of The Times is slammed down on to the adjacent seat.

"I didn't mean... what I did mean is that we are all affected and..."

"We most certainly are."

"It is tragic, certainly."

"Wouldn't go that far but an inconvenience one could have done without."

"I suppose we are lucky really though."

"Lucky. How does that compute?"

"Just that, you know, it could have been worse."

"How so?" Picks up a discarded newspaper and scans the

obituary column while cocking his head slightly to feign a still-listening position.

"Those people in the West Country have been trapped for weeks, haven't they? I mean we're used to having to make detours each winter when they flood Welney Wash but you don't expect it on the Somerset Levels do you?"

"I do not."

"The Thames bursting its banks is bad enough but with such saturated ground there are no means of pumping the flood water back into the river is there?"

"There isn't."

"Some people are saying that it's reached Biblical proportions – the amount of rain we've had – and others are even blaming it on God being unhappy and sending it as some kind of punishment."

"They would do."

"A bit far-fetched if you ask me."

"I didn't."

"I don't suppose you could sum it up in just a few words – what's gone wrong I mean. That heavy rain in the Pacific was supposed to have started the whole process off: sent the air stream to the north of the United States which in turn brought polar air down over the eastern seaboard that altered the course of our own jet stream across the Atlantic."

"It did."

"Causing the winds to push even harder. Of course, the

Global Warming crew are having a field day."

"They are."

"Warmer seas mean more water is absorbed into the atmosphere as clouds and that is why we are deluged by continuous storms. They say we've not had such an incidence of rainfall for two hundred and fifty years don't they?"

"They do."

"Should have brought the Dutch in earlier. Goodness knows they are the drainage experts. You don't have to actually drive out into the Fens to appreciate that."

"You don't."

"I really don't know where it's all going to end; honestly, I don't."

"With a plumber, presumably."

"I'm sorry I don't understand. How could one plumber make such a difference, or are you speaking religiously?"

"I am. You do often need to pray for one to arrive."

"One what?"

"A plumber! Have you not been listening to a word I've said? The burst water main in Ely this morning - flooded the car park off Barton Road. I had to drive all the way to Angel Drove."

TRAVELLING POST OFFICE

I often overhear (and, yes, actively listen in to) conversations between two or more people when travelling by train. Usually, it is because they are speaking too loud and are trying to impress fellow commuters such as me with their stories of great wealth or worthiness.

Sometimes, though, I am intrigued by the speakers themselves and how they process words or whole sentences in the way that they do.

Last week I found myself witnessing a comedy sketch that could have been written for the 'Alas Smith and Jones' television series. Truth often is stranger than fiction and I sometimes find myself questioning whether or not I am actually listening to actors rehearsing fictional lines.

"He used to work in the Travelling Post Office - or 'TPO' as they called it."

"Who did?"

"My father: seventeen years in total."

"I thought you said he worked for the Post Office, not an oil company."

"I never mentioned an oil company."

"Total; like *BP, Esso, Shell*..."

"Yes, yes. Thank you. I do know the names of the big petrol retailers too. It would have been *National* or *Regent* in his day - or even *Gainsborough*."

"French!"

"Sorry?"

"No need to be. I don't suppose they can help it. *Total*: it's actually French and spoken as 'Toetarl'"

"My father never liked the French very much; a good job the Channel Tunnel wasn't built then. I can't see him wanting to travel to a different country each night – Norwich, London or Crewe was bad enough. 'Oh, Mr Porter, what am I going to do...'"

"Who are you addressing? There's no porter on here is there?"

"No, I..."

"Is he working undercover?"

"No; it's a song '...I want to go to Birmingham but they're taking me on to Crewe.'"

"Heading to the wrong destination can be pretty traumatic. I know. I fell asleep once and didn't get off the train at Ely; snored all the way to King's Lynn and had to pay a fine."

"The mail carriages Dad travelled in were really narrow but at least he was guaranteed a seat for every journey."

"So where did they put the bikes?"

"What bikes?"

"Well, travelling postmen always have bikes or vans, don't they? I'm not stupid: they can't carry their vans on to railway carriages."

"He did bike around the local villages delivering the letters once upon a time."

"Before he realised it was faster by train I suppose."

"He missed the fresh air and the sunshine, to be honest. They used to sort letters right through the night, dropping heavy mailbags off at major stations on route so that they could be taken by road to village Post Offices; the local postmen would deliver them from there."

"I suppose that would have been for the best as not all houses have railway lines running behind them, do they?"

"Only model trains for small boys and old men to enjoy until life completes its circle and delivers the last post."

RENOVATION

"Yes Jacyntha, I do hear what you are saying; there's no need to shout. We'll see about some new crayons when we get to Cambridge. But Mummy is not promising; let's see how well you can behave first. Now, you sit there, with Toby in the seats behind me so that I can talk to GrandPa quietly."

"So, these are the plans Jeremy got through this morning. I thought you might like to see them."

"And so I would, but perhaps best to keep your voice down a bit?"

"Sorry. Sorry. Just excited I suppose. Not often you get the chance to renovate an old vicarage, God help us! Oh! Ha ha ha ha… so there's the main room. It's divided into two sitting rooms at present…"

"Decent size though and…"

"Exactly. Exactly. Jeremy thought we might keep that wall."

"It's a supporting wall so you might have to!"

"Exactly! This is the reception hall which will be so useful. I mean I really like the idea of it and love the reality…"

"A lot of work though, especially with two young children to look after?"

"I know. I know. We're looking at boarding places as well,

obviously."

"So soon?"

"Well, we can't keep them at home alone – not that we'll have much cash for anything other than screwing from now on – but we've found a few possibilities nearby. There's the persistent smell of poo to contend with, naturally, but regular dry food and water: all you can ask for really."

"Please tell me you are not talking about the children here."

"Ha. Ha ha ha. Of course not, you old silly. I do really believe you're losing it, Pa."

"Not so loud!"

"Sorry. Just couldn't help it. No, the cats haven't even been told we're moving yet. Not sure how they'll take it."

"Lying down I suppose?"

"...which brings us nicely on to the bedrooms: three, but sadly no en-suite. I suppose vicars didn't mind padding along corridors in bare feet and hair shirts, but I can't live with that. Jeremy was ahead of me and said we should pray that the listing doesn't stop us knocking the old place into shape."

"Grade 2 I expect?"

"No idea. Jeremy knows - he was the one who did history; said there were lots of medieval covenants to deal with, but he saw no reason why we couldn't look into converting - the attics that is. I mean it frightens me a little bit, it really does, but I love the reality... what? What's this? Oh, a dear little drawing of the new house. Golly, you've captured it really rather well - hasn't she Grandpa?"

"We'll make an artist out of you yet, or maybe even an architect like your poor old GrandPa…"

"So, this is a morning room. Jeremy is already calling it a G&T den though…"

"Surely more of a drawing room?"

"Exactly. She's so good at drawing, isn't she? No idea where that talent comes from…"

ALLERGY

Platform 2, Ely Station. 8.50 AM

Lady One (wearing a maroon skirt and black, sleeveless top): "This is the disconnect, you see. I mean they were perfectly understanding on the 'phone – a bit, you know, Italian - but then, when we got there…"

Lady Two (wearing a black skirt and maroon, sleeveless top): "Oh, don't get me started on the 'phone…"

Lady Two's mobile 'phone rings

Lady Three (wearing a maroon dress with black jacket): "I'm feeling quite coordinated today, ladies!"

Lady Two: "No. No that is not what I asked you to do."

Lady One: "The uniforms at the restaurant were fine. The welcome was fine. Everything was fine until we came to order…"

Lady Two: "Are we clear? I don't want to get there and find that I've just been talking to myself again."

Lady Three: "I've always liked maroon as a colour; less delicate than pink of course but then again so are we!"

Lady One: "We went patiently through the menu options and the waiter appeared to understand what we were trying to communicate to him."

Lady Two (hurling mobile 'phone in Olympic-sized blue handbag): "Why don't people just listen; I mean how difficult can it be?"

Lady One: "I should have realised that we had an issue, even then. I mean he was charming enough, but he was a temp. You could tell by the way he held his notepad."

"Lady Three: "I hope we get a seat today. I only get the 8.58 because it's cheaper but not sure it's worth the saving if we have to stand like we did yesterday. At least I'm not alone."

Lady One: "So we chose pizza. He doesn't really like pizza but the only other thing they did was pasta. The waiter wrote it all down – or at least I assume that's what he was doing with his pencil: Margherita with no cheese and no tomato."

Lady Two: "Too excitable. That's the issue. Their minds are on one thing and one thing only."

Lady One: "I explained about his allergy."

Lady Three: "Late again! Personally, I blame the station announcer."

Lady One: "So imagine my surprise when he finally came."

Lady Two: "Young boys. Cook up a storm given half a chance."

Lady One: "What's this? I said. I was quite calm at that stage, assuming there was some mix-up."

Lady Three: "Bad news is so straightforward isn't it: clinical somehow? There's no room for 'what if' or 'could it be' it's just exactly what it is. Hard to bear."

Lady Two: "I told him. No more games it's time for bed. I'm not usually disappointed."

Lady One: "And he just glared at me. I mean - glared."

Lady Three: "Like colours really. Hopeful of a better day ahead but with a dark shadow over everything."

Lady One: "So I glared back and then just went off on one."

Lady Two: "Me too."

Lady One: "He has an allergy."

Lady Two: "Quite."

Lady One: "He cannot eat basil; comprendez?"

COMMONWEALTH

A small white girl of about nine or ten sits next to Father on the early morning train to London. A middle-aged man of Asian origin sits opposite her; a West Indian family with two smaller children sit across the aisle from them.

She is wearing pink shorts below a simple white tee shirt and looks suntanned and cool.

He is dressed in a dark blue suit and grey silk tie over a plain white shirt. In his 'forties, he looks pale, hot and sweaty.

"Daddy?"

"Yes, darling."

"Before you go back to your Metro can you explain to me what the Commonwealth is, please?"

"Shhh. Not so loud. Which bit didn't you understand? We spent over half an hour talking about this on the journey to the station."

"I didn't get the bit about the smutty man."

Asian man lifts his head from The Times and smiles slightly as he too anticipates the answer.

"There is – was – no smut! There was a man called Jan Smuts who was from South Africa..."

"Where the rich white people still live off of the gold that the poor black people dig out of the ground?"

"Yes, well not exactly. I wouldn't put it quite like that."

Furtive glances from West Indian man.

"But that's what you said!"

"I think there are a lot of issues in that country still."

"Because of the cold?"

"Sorry?"

"The cold. Lots of people must have colds if they need so many tissues."

Asian man goes back to his paper while West Indian man chuckles aloud.

"No, darling. Issues – things that need sorting out – not tissues."

"But if you had a cold, you'd need a tissue to sort out your nose?"

"Let's just forget about tissues, shall we?"

"Are you alright Daddy? You look a bit hot."

"I'm fine, thank you. Just keep your voice down a bit."

"So, what did the smutty man say?"

"Not smutty! Smuts. His name was Smuts, and he first came up with the name: 'British Commonwealth of Nations;' we tend to just call it the Commonwealth now though."

"Because we don't own the other countries anymore."

Asian man and West Indian man and women glance at

Father.

"We never actually owned them, darling; they're not like toys."

"But you said that the British Empire once ruled the whole world and now only a few bits are left which we have to call the Commonwealth because we had to share them out!"

"Well, I don't think I actually said…"

"And the Queen is just a gingerbread."

West Indian children look up from their crossword books.

"No, a figurehead, darling, not a gingerbread."

"Phew, that's a good job; she might have melted away in the rain otherwise!"

"Hopefully not. All the Commonwealth nations would be very upset if that happened!"

"I thought you said they couldn't wait to get rid of us?"

"Well, I…"

The train stops at Royston and Asian man alights, addressing Father as he does so:

"Enjoy the 'Friendly' Games."

BRUNCH

Two round ladies roll on to the train at Ely at the precise moment the doors begin to close. One only makes it halfway.

"Oh no. Stupid…"

"Excuse me! Excuse me! Hello. My friend is stuck here can you help please?"

"The alarm is there for a reason, madam, and safety notices are posted…"

"Yes. Yes, but this is an emergency. The train is about to move and she's only wearing plimsolls…"

"I can assure you that nobody will be leaving this station until I am satisfied that all Health and Safety procedures have been completed and…"

"Fine. That's great. Can you just open the doors please!"

"Joan. My coffee. I can't hold on much longer. I can feel it slipping through my fingers."

"It's alright. Let go – gradually. There, I'll just pop it down on the floor here."

"But it might fall over."

"I'll keep an eye on it."

"It's got three sugars in it…"

"Why doesn't he open the doors? Excuse me!"

"Yes madam."

"Any progress?"

"As I said, I am completing my safety checks."

"Having a woman stuck out sideways from one of the carriage doors can't be safe, can it? Anyone can see that!"

"And perhaps anyone could have seen it coming, madam!"

"I may have to have a croissant, after all, Joan. I know we said we'd wait until Letchworth but I don't think I'm going to make it."

"Stay where you are, Ruth. We can do this or rather he can."

The doors open and Ruth slumps to the floor. Exhausted, she is hauled into the train by Joan.

"Thank you – eventually."

"Don't thank me, madam, thank the Board of Abellio Greater Anglia for providing a framework in which passenger safety is held…"

The doors close again.

"No wonder the trains never run on time."

"He did save my life, Joan. Just in time too. This coffee's only lukewarm now."

"And no seats of course. Why don't they provide longer trains? If they did, we wouldn't have had to rush up the platform and you wouldn't have had your accident."

"At least we have food and drink."

"If they were really serious about Health and Safety, they'd put on longer trains so that people didn't have to walk so far."

"Especially as we had to walk all the way under that tunnel as well. I don't really understand why to be honest. I mean surely most people want to go to London for the shopping. King's Lynn doesn't really compare, does it? It would suit me much better if all the trains came in on Platform One, next to the L.A. Golden Bean café."

"I wonder if the L.A. really does refer to Los Angeles?"

"Los Angeles? In America? That's amazing, Joan. All that way away! Makes you wonder how they keep it all fresh doesn't it?"

"I bet they don't hide behind bureaucracy either!"

"And their customers will be much happier: eating, drinking and not having to travel so far."

CHARGE

The 17.14 (quarter-past five was never going to be sophisticated enough for 'railway time') to Ely has come to a standstill.

It left on time, so no compensation charges can be levied on Great Northern Trains just yet. It is still 'great' but only just. During the 1.3 minutes that we have been resting peacefully in the Hertfordshire countryside, many of the customers packed into seats and aisles are already becoming restless.

It's not that the aspect ratio isn't good: "large wall-to-wall windows with triple glazing, offering fantastic views over rolling fields and providing excellent transport links…." It isn't even that it is especially hot as the weather has deteriorated with autumn's fall and consequently the carriage heating has been turned off. It is because individuals have suddenly realised that they are not travelling alone and don't like what they now see and hear all around them.

An extremely important man in his mid-forties, dressed in sharp, dark suit and still crisp white shirt (how do people manage this after a full day's work?) has been tapping away at his laptop beside me since he first took his seat having first glanced over at me, ever so subtly, to make sure I was no threat to his sartorial domination. That is never likely to happen so he could have just stared.

Opposite us sit two elderly ladies, one hitherto lost to her Kindle (violent crime or rampant sex I suspect) while her friend, similarly groomed and rouged and scarved has probably read two pages of her old-fashioned paperback, judging by the lack of page-turning and drooping eyelids.

When the train came to its sudden, unscheduled stop, the ladies looked up in disgust, sniffed disdainfully and proceeded to fidget, as though their very beings were under attack by the railway company. The paperback non-reader had already been affronted by the extremely important man's laptop being placed carefully (in his lap for goodness's sake!) so that it came to between one and two feet of touching her soul. What I know that she doesn't is that he is actually playing an online version of PacMan and will continue to try to gobble up fruit until he loses the signal (or patience) on the approach to Royston.

His mobile 'phone suddenly rings – the 'Dance of the Knights' theme sounds a stark contrast to his online grocery quest and 'Juliet' and her friend make dramatic, exaggerated sighs and shift their ample forms in the seats that bind them to this scene.

"No. No, I didn't get your messages I'm afraid. I've been in the office all day. Still am in fact."

They both look up and simultaneously roll their eyes even higher.

"What noise? Oh, just a few of the other staff milling around; most have left for the day."

Silence and then, totally unexpectedly and quite wonderfully, the two women begin to sing at the tops of their voices:

"You're not fit, you're not fit, you're not fit to be in charge."

HAPPY NEW YEAR

"Happy New Year!"

"Thank you; the same to you. Sounds a bit odd now though, doesn't it? On what day in January does it become inappropriate to say such things: it's the Ninth of January already…"

"I suppose it's a force of habit really – you know - when you see someone for the first time after Christmas."

"Unless it's before New Year's Eve of course!"

"Haha. I suppose every day is before a New Year's Eve in some strange way?"

"Or after it…"

"Shall I put your bag up on the rack?"

"No. No that's quite alright, thanks."

"You're not going all the way to London then?"

"Sorry? Oh, I see what you mean – yes, yes, I am down for the day. I still have some preparation to do though."

"Well, I won't keep you…"

"That's fine. I also have a skinny latte Grande to finish!"

"Funny the names they give them these days, isn't it? In our day it was tea or coffee and sometimes a hot chocolate if you were feeling exotic!"

"Quite; although I am a little younger than you, remember."

"Of course. Of course. Mind you, imagine if the café waitress in *Brief Encounter* had today's drinks options to offer – it certainly wouldn't be brief, would it?"

"I'm afraid I don't know the film..."

"A classic of its kind!"

"But not worn so well as 'classics' such as *Great Expectations* or *The Fighting Temeraire*?"

"I don't know the last one I'm afraid, but I saw the first again over Christmas – well you have to don't you? What a fine director David Lean was."

"I'm sure. Ah well..."

"Some of the scenes in *Brief Encounter* took place in a café at the station tea shop. Not like the vending booths or soulless waiting room at Cambridge: a proper tea shop."

"With a limited choice of tea, coffee and chocolate no doubt."

"Yes, but it had such character. Then the officious waitress starts asking if he – Alec, who is a doctor at the local hospital - wants large or small, sugar or no sugar..."

"Sounds captivating."

"While Laura's head is in a complete whirl. She is excited by the possibility of change but simultaneously fights it. Her conscience wins in the end, and she returns to her husband – Fred, I think his name was – and children; but they were that close to having an affair. The endless questioning just raises the tension."

"I'm afraid films aren't really my thing…"

"Celia Johnson and Trevor Howard. Both long dead now of course."

"But the memory lives on…"

"I guess affairs happen all the time these days; the statistics certainly suggest it."

"What an old-fashioned word! I'm sure that marriage is far less of a prison than it once was - if that's what you mean."

"I've never been married so films have become my best friends I suppose."

"I really do have to work now."

"Of course. Once again: Happy New Year to you."

UNITED

"Seven hours it took us!" An earnest young man expels the giveaway garlic aroma of last night's microwaved lasagne as he recalls and shares yet again his team's expulsion from the FA Cup with anyone who can still stomach it.

He is dressed in a cheap grey suit and chews noisily on at least one croissant while simultaneously attempting to throw take-away tea into the same goal.

"Manchester isn't that far away, surely?" His travelling companion – or victim, who had the misfortune to make eye contact and is now suffering the same consequences as Cambridge United did – is older, quietly spoken and not bursting out of his own skin through pies or enthusiasm.

"Not as the crow flies, no, but crows don't have to follow the M6 do they?"

"I thought there was a toll road at Birmingham now?"

"Packed that was. People have more money than sense if you ask me."

The wise man doesn't and so the young adventurer continues (to eat as well as talk):

"We got stuck near Walsall first; then Litchfield?"

"Beautiful cathedral and of course there's the Chase at Cannock."

"Looked like a bit of a dump to me and I've never been one for horseracing."

"It's a beautiful part of the country, actually.

"That's as maybe but we saw just a bit too much of it; know what I mean? We weren't planning to stay there, just drive through it to get to the match. It's like on here. You don't get the train every morning to admire the fields, do you?"

"Well…"

"I mean they're not going to be going anywhere are they – a bit like us on Tuesday!" He laughs out loud at his own attempt at wit while looking around the carriage for knowing smiles of encouragement. Spotting only blank faces looking downward – even those without newspapers or tablets or books – he removes a final croissant from its brown paper bag before nonchalantly screwing it up and hurling it under his seat.

Resisting the urge to retrieve it, the older man - visibly weary now of the hour and the man – settles back into his seat but good manners oblige him to continue the conversation if only to end it correctly.

"So, did you get to Old Trafford in time?"

"Nah! They had to delay the kick-off. A pity really."

"Because you still missed the start?"

"Oh no. We got into the ground just in time to see Elliott hit the post. Thing is I wanted to have a few beers first - you know - soak up the atmosphere!"

"There were over six thousand from Cambridge, I think I read?"

"Dunno. Nightmare getting out of the car park afterwards. I do know that."

"Must have been worth it though? I mean, what a great experience: travelling away with your mates; cheering on the local team."

"I suppose so. I went on my own so not really that different from being packed into a train full of strangers."

ELECTION

Two 'young professional' men in their mid-twenties are sitting in a section of four seats on the packed 7.22 from Ely to Cambridge.

A middle-aged couple has managed to push through the group of fellow passengers who have similarly pushed those in front of them on to the train but then chosen to stand right in front of the closing door – as if to prevent others from following their examples.

"Excuse me but do you think we could sit there?" The elderly man is sweating over bushy grey eyebrows and beard. His baggy pink anorak gives the impression that they have been invaded by an enormous wobbly jelly.

"And where do you propose that we go? The train is rather busy, in case you hadn't noticed." The gentleman pulls his suit jacket closer – presumably to keep out the germs – and turns to gaze out of the window.

There is a sharp intake of breath from the woman; less Womble than her husband but sporting a full head of grey hair which meanders down to her all-encompassing blue, knitted sweater.

"It's just that we have our grand-daughter and her friend with us. There are four of us, you see, and these sections are really meant for families." The elderly man tries again.

Both gentlemen look around to try and identify the grand spawn of two such fine individuals but spy no obvious candidate, not even hidden from view by the sweater.

"Why don't you two take the seats next to us and then take it in turns to let your granddaughter sit... once she comes?"

They do so obediently, facing each other and ignoring the stifled giggles beside them.

"I suppose we must expect five more years of this then?" She addresses this seemingly random thought to her husband.

Their travelling companions exchange knowing glances before staring smugly out of the window at a young woman who is struggling to get a pushchair on to the adjacent train.

"Bet she didn't consider that outcome when she was all dressed up on a Friday night!" The two laugh out loud while simultaneously checking their iPhone screens.

"And what sort of outcome would that be?" A booming voice from the aisle stops all of them in their tracks – even the train although, technically, it hasn't left the station yet.

The grandparents continue to look at each other impassively but both gentlemen immediately look sideways to find a tall woman of about their age, dressed in a black leather jacket and dirty jeans. But it is her thick-set companion, head bent to follow the curve of the carriage roof, who really alarms them. Dressed in similar bikers' leather with the unmistakable Hells Angels motif on his jacket he is glaring at both of them and eventually growls:

"Further welfare cuts for the old and the young may

be justified by previous policies of overspending, but common decency is priceless. We'll discuss it further – democratically of course - whenever and wherever you choose to disembark."

NEWS TRAVELS

I consult for a company called Newsworks. Based in London it is the marketing body for national newspapers 'in all their forms.' The word, therefore, describing this better than newspapers is 'newsbrands' which, according to the latest research, reach almost twenty million people in the UK every day.

Naturally, my mind is focused on newsbrands whenever I travel down for meetings, and I find myself looking around the packed railway carriage to observe my fellow travellers' consumption of news. I could be rather grand and call it 'consumer research' but it's me just being nosy really.

Two weeks ago, I muscled my way on to the train at Ely and eventually found an empty seat – or at least one where the only occupant was a rucksack belonging to a young lad, dressed in jeans and jumper and thus already sweating in the muggy conditions (the boy not the rucksack).

"Do you mind if I sit down?" I asked cheerily, not really caring if he did or not – why do we ask such fatuous questions? (Last week I asked a bedraggled woman if it was still raining outside as she dripped her way up the aisle).

"Of course not!" he replied, removing the sleeping item to the luggage rack while almost making room for me to squeeze past, sitting as he was at forty-five degrees to the window. As I made to finish my paper copy of the Metro newspaper he leaned over my right arm and started to read the stories with me simultaneously - I guess this is what they mean by 'reach?' Unfortunately, he was quite a slow reader and 'tutted' ever so slightly each time I turned the page.

We then heard a middle-aged woman in a bright pink dress announce loudly from the seat in front of us that at least 2,600 sick and disabled people had died after being declared fit to work and taken off benefits. I saw that she was reading Mail Online on her tablet which I thought was a surprising leader for that particular newspaper but, no, she wasn't reading the story upside down.

This was too much for my reading partner who hopped off at Waterbeach to be replaced by an extremely important man - probably in his early sixties - wearing a three-piece blue suit and definitely exhibiting the smellier results of sweat.

I expected a Telegraph or at least a Times to appear from his old-fashioned brown, leather briefcase which he had kindly placed below his legs and mine but was surprised to see another paper Metro appear – even more so when I realised it was the previous day's edition.

I opened my tablet version of the Guardian and was now unobtrusively able to read the football reports when I saw my neighbour ringing yesterdays' news stories.

I handed him my Metro from that day, but he merely shrugged and declared officiously:

"Nobody could say that Iain Duncan Smith didn't have it coming."

LOBSTERS

"Yeah, yeah. I can now. Signal quite poor but less disruption in the carriage now, thank God. I suspect many of the unwashed will disembark in Cambridge. Yeah…yeah, absolutely!! Sorry, oh, look, sorry – got another call coming in I'd better take. Sure. Yeah, yeah…cool."

"Hello. Well, I was on a pretty important call, to be honest. What do you want? OK well, get on to the dairy then. No… no, just point out that we ordered semi-skimmed and that's what we need. I'm not really interested in the mechanics of milk floats, to be honest… well, you'll have to seek an alternative supply from the Co-op then!

We can't serve them indigestible lactose, or they might be up half the night, messing up the new tiles. No! Skimmed looks as though we've been watering the stuff down. Only get a two-pint carton though – we don't want to be left with a milk lake. Remember, this is really, really important to us.

What? Like I said last night, Lidl has them on offer: £4.95. Of course, they are! Lobsters are lobsters. We'll use that Shloer we got from Asda… of course they don't! Against their religion. Do I really need to spell all of this out? I'll silently sink my claws in while you talk to her about lip gloss or something. It really isn't that difficult. Sorry? What outstanding amount? OK: phone the electricity company and ask them to come and re-check the meter. At the top of the bill, I expect! Anything else? Right."

"Sorry Charles – little woman fussing over whatever they waste their days fussing over! Indeed! Sure. Sure. No, it will all be fine. Be assured that I've done my due diligence on them. She's from Iraq, isn't she? Oh, well next-door neighbours at least! Yes, I've already crafted something to go out tomorrow morning, but my feeling is that we need to situate this very carefully in order to effect a formal introduction. It needs to look externally as though we are tough and confident in our expectation of success for the project. Cool.

Yeah...yeah. As I understand it tonight is really about us taking an opportune moment to create a backchannel should we need to change our colours and move sideways a little in order to then move forward again. I'm sorry Charles - lost you to 3G for a moment – does he? Righty-ho, No, no problem at all. All in hand... they don't? Neither of them? OK. Yeah, yeah. Flexibility is why I was attracted to the service in the first place so... yes, of course. You can rely on me. Yeah, yeah. Cool. I'll report back tomorrow. I will. Thanks, Charles. Bye...bye."

"It's me again. Change of plan. Apparently, he owns a vineyard out there. God knows how they survive the heat or His contempt for them. What? No matter, just a play on... never mind! Another slight problem is that neither of them eats seafood. What? Start praying..."

EXTRAORDINARY, DARLING

"He was marvellous of course: directed me in my first Hamlet, you know... pity they can't advertise cigars now but it was a nice little earner at the time!"

A booming laugh followed this booming voice - with extended highlights broadcast at regular intervals between Royston and Letchworth. The otherwise diminutive man in his late 60's was soberly dressed in dark coat and jeans, but the white cap and yellow silk scarf should have been a giveaway when I was choosing my seat which backed on to his.

"I always say that you should treasure those periods between contracts, don't you? I mean without those breaks – those quiet times – one would hardly have time to recover. I was truly exhausted after Pinter."

This was no theatre in the round so I couldn't see who these soundbites were being aimed at; whether that unfortunate (former) acquaintance was asleep – or, indeed, whether they actually existed at all.

"He had an extraordinary little flat in Soho you know. Did you ever visit? That reminds me of our time in Wrexham! Do you remember the aspidistra?"

Heads turned. Faces that seemed previously featureless now came into sharp, pained relief. He was clearly reaching his audience.

"Just wasn't for me, darling. I mean pantomime is for piers isn't it, not professionals. Mind you, I did love his Puss. Now, where was I? Ah, yes: the rep tour in '58…"

Ah.

"Of course, in those days one really had to work at one's craft. Today it's all about editing and post-production but having a gift back then just wasn't sufficient, was it? The stage was bare, and we had to dress it, transform it really. Jolly hard work too. I'm not surprised so many fell by the wayside. How did the teaching career work out by the way?"

"Please be aware that this is a non-stopping service to London King's Cross."

The supporting driver delivered his line loudly (if a little muffled) but there was silence from our actor's imaginary friend. Perhaps they had choked or been simply speechless. No matter: the show had to go on, so he continued to ad lib professionally:

"I assume railway personnel are selected on the basis of their inability to speak proper English! Well, you'd know all about that from the classrooms I suppose. It doesn't ever really leave you, does it? Performing as a character I mean? Being stripped naked by prying eyes would be simply impossible without training although I did have some run-ins with one or two members, I can tell you!"

A recent joiner from Letchworth – a burly man with early

morning attitude – was less inclined to hear about them:

"Can you keep the noise down please mate. Some of us just want a bit of quiet."

"A bit of hush, is it? Well, fine by me darling although, as Larry once said to me: 'we are a long time quiet, now is the time for words, not inaction.' Extraordinary don't you think?

CENTRE COURT

"I just don't think, you know, as my husband might say, that it's really cricket."

A woman in her late fifties is sitting in the aisle seat just across from me with her rather large, slightly older lady friend wedged in against the window. Glasses placed carefully on expensively coiffured but not that luxurious copper hair which might once have been mousy and blonde, her long leg is extended into the aisle. Tantalisingly balanced on a knee just hidden by tight-fitting dark leather (or plastic?) skirt, the leg continually moves through an exaggerated arc, lest we should all think about something - well, anything - else for even a fleeting moment.

"Sorry, Delia?"

The much frumpier friend (perhaps a last-minute designer accessory?) is struggling to fit the remains of an over-ripe peach through her rouged lips, without the consequent juice spurting out all over her faded floral blouse and spoiling the effect of being made-up.

"I thought you were talking about the tennis!"

"Indeed."

Delia drawls a response in a voice perceived to resemble honey but sounding more like vinaigrette. Observing that she (surely not they?) is being observed from a facing seat by a rotund middle-aged man in a bright blue blazer, she treats all of us to a languid crossing of her legs as if we are meant to consider a changing of the balls according to the tennis metaphors we are bound to be inhabiting.

"My point was that there were so many untidy people at Wimbledon yesterday. You know: inappropriately dressed."

The friend considers this after a quick but not unseen replay of the point reveals that the perspiration on the tramlines of her outfit has indeed been joined by peach juice on the dry and worn centre court.

"Did you get tickets yesterday, then? To the Andy Murray match?"

Increasingly hopeful of an intrigue between her and blazer man, Delia is momentarily knocked out of her stride by such a surprising backhand return. She takes a rather ingenious comfort break to sensually redo her own subtly pink lipstick, making sure that she is in position for a baseline serve before delivering it.

"My husband could have got a pair, obviously, but we had a previous engagement so no, we ended up watching it in the lounge with Pimms and bits. So much easier than the hike down to town!"

Whether it is the thought of alcohol or food or lying on a sofa with Delia, blazer man leans forward suddenly as if to anticipate a further volley at the net. But the friend has a break point and knows that she has had few enough opportunities in her life up until this moment; this defining moment of the open era.

"We watched it in bed actually. I always get so excited when

I see so much flesh, especially those muscly legs. Honestly, I could have played the bagpipes when Andy came through, and yet I've never been trained darling; you know, never."

HAIRY JOURNEY

I had a meeting in London at 11.00 this morning but my preferred train – the 8.58 from Ely (mainly because it's the first 'cheap' one I can catch in the mornings) – has been unreliable lately and therefore the onward Tube journey from King's Cross to Hyde Park Corner cut things a bit fine so that I have been minutes late on more than one occasion.

So, I decided to get an earlier train which, coupled with the need to grab a space in the 'overflow' car park - which itself overflows if more than about fifteen car drivers decide to park there – and the icy morning, saw me get up at 5.30 and leave the house at 6.15. I am therefore allowing nearly five hours for my journey in order not to be late for my 11 o'clock meeting by a few minutes.

I paid a premium rate for the privilege of a 'peak time journey' and ran through the tunnel at Ely Station to ensure that I could see the 6.47 leave just as the still dark skies reminded me how absurdly early it all was.

I then sat in silence with other cold and frustrated failures until the 7.22 arrived. The 6.47 has 12 carriages but, because we then move closer to normal working hours, Great Northern cleverly supplies only 8 carriages for this train in a breath-taking display of counter-intuition.

The result is, of course, massive overcrowding – and the train had so far only come from King's Lynn. I fought my way to the end of the rows of seats so that I at least had some space to stand in.

Flanked on either side by 'lucky' customers who were sitting in the 'special luggage racks provided' and could thus be transported like the cattle each railway franchise truly considers us to be, I looked back down the carriage and, apart from the far-away customers grinning smugly at me from their facing seats by the door, each one of the other seated customers was facing away from me.

It proved to be a very interesting experiment in that, without any facial clues or (obviously) verbal clues to break the silence, the only indications of personality were the backs of peoples' heads and hair types.

I quickly came to the following conclusions:

There is something extremely unpleasant about holding on to the edge of someone's seat for balance and feeling their hair on your fingers as they lean back luxuriantly;

Dandruff is alive and kicking and readily shared with fellow passengers whenever someone shakes their head;

Fierce spots and boils – even when uniformly placed on the neck – are not a great look;

Grey ponytails on men over fifty should, like all ponies everywhere, be let loose and take their chances.

My Dad used to say that the backs of your shoes were key and needed extra polish. Is each day a bad hair day for most people? If so, they need to pull their socks up.

The End

MAILING LIST

If you enjoyed this book, please rate it on Amazon.

Please also join our mailing list for the latest news, including about forthcoming books.

ABOUT THE AUTHOR

Mark Rasdall

Mark Rasdall was born in Peterborough in 1960 and brought up on the edge of the Cambridgeshire Fens. A writer of fiction and history, with a professional background in content creation, curation, and online search in London's advertising sector, he is based in the UK, in a small village on top of a hill in the beautiful Worcestershire countryside. For a few years he ran a sweet shop on Worcester High Street with his wife Michelle.

Now retired, he writes fiction and history books.

You can visit his website at www.markrasdallwriting.com and follow Mark on Facebook, Instagram, X and Bluesky

Printed in Great Britain
by Amazon